If You Go with Your Goat to VOTE

written by **Jan Zauzmer**

illustrated by **Andrew Roberts**

THE EXPERIMENT
NEW YORK

The Experiment, LLC
220 East 23rd Street, Suite 600
New York, NY 10010-4658
theexperimentpublishing.com

THE EXPERIMENT and its colophon are registered trademarks of The Experiment, LLC. Many of the designations used by manufacturers and sellers to distinguish their products are claimed as trademarks. Where those designations appear in this book and The Experiment was aware of a trademark claim, the designations have been capitalized.

The Experiment's books are available at special discounts when purchased in bulk for premiums and sales promotions as well as for fund-raising or educational use. For details, contact us at info@theexperimentpublishing.com.

Library of Congress Cataloging-in-Publication Data available upon request

ISBN 978-1-61519-746-0
Ebook ISBN 978-1-61519-747-7

Cover and text design by Beth Bugler

Manufactured in China

First printing September 2020
10 9 8 7 6 5 4 3 2 1

If you are a kid and you go with your goat to vote . . .

you may chew
over the ballot.

If you are a duckling and you
go with your drake to vote . . .

you may make a splash when you
send in your picks by snail mail.

If you are a bunny
and you go with your
rabbit to vote . . .

WHALE
of a
CANDIDATE

the
BUCK
STOPS
HERE

GIVE
FLEAS
A
CHANCE

WE
-the-
ANIMALS

TOP
DOG

STARS
AND
STRIPES

LEADING THE PACK

STAND TALL

I LIKE PIKE

you may hop to the polling place on Election Day.

VOTE HERE →

LET'S TALK TURKEY

SEAL THE DEAL

If you are a puggle and you go with your platypus to vote . . .

you may find that
a snack fits the bill
while you wait in line.

If you are a hatchling and you
go with your turtle to vote . . .

you may come out of your shell at the sign-in desk.

If you are a joey
and you go with
your kangaroo to vote . . .

you may jump for joy
when it's your turn to
enter the booth.

If you are a gosling and you go
with your gander to vote . . .

you may get goose bumps when
you see the list of candidates.

If you are a small fry and you go with your octopus to vote . . .

you may marvel as she
inks in the bubbles.

If you are a tadpole and you go
with your bullfrog to vote . . .

you may leap at
the chance to help
push the buttons.

If you are a piglet and you
go with your hog to vote . . .

you may squeal with delight when you get an "I Voted" sticker.

If you are a peachick and you go with your peacock to vote . . .

you may proudly strut your stuff as you head back home.

If you are a porcupette and you go
with your porcupine to vote . . .

you may be on pins
and needles as the
results come in.

If you are an owlet and you
go with your owl to vote . . .

you may stay up late because
you give a hoot about who wins.

If you are a kid and you go with your grown-up to vote . . .

you will grow up to vote
yourself—no kidding!